Brave Dragon

WITHDRAWN

By Bill Scollon
Based on the episode "Un-Burr-Able," written by Kent Redeker
Based on the series created by Chris Nee
Illustrated by Character Building Studio and the Disney Storybook Art Team

ABDOPUBLISHING.COM

Reinforced library bound edition published in 2019 by Spotlight, a division of ABDO, PO Box 398166, Minneapolis, Minnesota 55439. Spotlight produces high-quality reinforced library bound editions for schools and libraries. Published by agreement with Disney Press, an imprint of Disney Book Group.

Printed in the United States of America, North Mankato, Minnesota.
042018   092018

DISNEP PRESS
New York • Los Angeles

THIS BOOK CONTAINS
RECYCLED MATERIALS

Library of Congress Control Number: 2017961151

Publisher's Cataloging in Publication Data

Names: Scollon, Bill, author. | Redeker, Kent, author. | Character Building Studio; Disney Storybook Art Team, illustrators.
Title: Doc McStuffins: Brave dragon / by Bill Scollon and Kent Redeker; illustrated by Character Building Studio and Disney Storybook Art Team.
Description: Minneapolis, MN : Spotlight, 2019 | Series: World of reading level pre-1
Summary: While playing with Doc and the other toys, Stuffy falls and gets covered in prickly burs. Doc fixes him, but something is wrong. Stuffy doesn't want to play! Can Doc help Stuffy become a brave dragon again?
Identifiers: ISBN 9781532141751 (lib. bdg.)
Subjects: LCSH: Doc McStuffins (Television program)--Juvenile fiction. | Stuffed animals (Toys)--Juvenile fiction. | Dragons--Juvenile fiction. | Cockleburs--Juvenile fiction. | Readers (Primary)--Juvenile fiction.
Classification: DDC [E]--dc23

Spotlight
A Division of ABDO
abdopublishing.com

The park is sunny.

Time to play!

Doc swings.
Whee!

Lambie runs.
Zoom!

Hallie is up.

Buddy is down.

Chilly slides.
Whoosh!

Stuffy jumps.
Wow!

The jump scared Stuffy.
"Be a brave dragon," says Doc.

"Brave dragon! Brave dragon!"
says Stuffy.

Time to play a game.

Kick the ball past Stuffy. Hit the pail!

Hallie kicks.

Stuffy catches.

Doc kicks.

Stuffy falls down.

Uh-oh! Stuffy is hurt.

He has bumps. Ouch!

"Be a brave dragon," says Doc.

"Brave dragon! Brave dragon!"
says Stuffy.

The bumps are gone. Hooray!

Time to play!

Lambie kicks.

Stuffy does not catch.
Uh-oh!

Stuffy is scared.

He may fall down.

He may get hurt.

But Stuffy wants to play.

"Be a brave dragon," says Doc.

"Brave dragon! Brave dragon!"
says Stuffy.

Stuffy hits the pail.
The brave dragon wins!

31901063643409